COUNTING
ARIZONA'S
Treasures

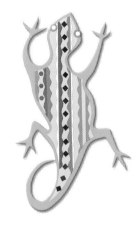

Text copyright © 2003 by Terri Fields
Photographs copyright © 2003 by Tony Marinella

Library of Congress Cataloging-in-Publication Data

Fields, Terri, 1948-
  Counting Arizona's treasures / by Terri Fields ; photography by Tony
Marinella.
        p. cm.
Summary: Lizards from ten to one visit some of Arizona's scenic and
man-made attractions. Includes a separate section with information on
the sites mentioned.
  ISBN 1-885772-03-3
  [1. Arizona--Description and travel--Fiction. 2. Lizards--Fiction. 3.
Counting. 4. Stories in rhyme.] I. Marinella, Tony, ill. II. Title.
  PZ8.3.F459Co 2003
  [E]--dc21
                                                        2003001223

Design by Rudy J. Ramos
Prepress: Ali Graphic Services Inc.
Printed in Hong Kong.

9 8 7 6 5 4 3 2 1

Kiva Publishing
Walnut, CA

To Rick, Jeff, Lori, Larry, Mom, Teri Golden and Suzi Scher,
who make all Arizona adventures so much fun.

And with special thanks to Donna Cook,
whose creative muse always shines brightly.

COUNTING

ARIZONA'S
Treasures

by **Terri Fields**   *photography by* **Tony Marinella**

Ten little lizards who
loved to run and play

Came to Arizona on
a sun-filled day.

10 Ten little lizards stood at Copper Queen Mine.

One left for Sedona,
and then there were nine.

9 Nine little lizards went up to Snowbowl's gate.

One left for Grand Canyon,
and then there were eight.

8 Eight little lizards thought Old Tucson was heaven.

 **One took off for Tombstone, and then there were seven.**

7

Seven little lizards saw
Jerome's ghostly tricks.

One left for London Bridge,
and then there were six.

Six little lizards took a big Lake Powell dive.

**One left for Colossal Cave,
and then there were five.**

Five little lizards went through Biosphere's door.

One left for Sabino,
and then there were four.

4 Four little lizards looked at a petrified tree.

One left for Kartchner Caverns,
and then there were three.

3 Three little lizards went to the big Phoenix Zoo.

One left for Heard Museum, and then there were two.

2 Two little lizards had some
Science Center fun.

One left for Walnut Canyon,
and then there was one.

1

One little lizard stayed in Phoenix for a day

**So he'd have time enough to sun
and swim and play.**

Then ten little lizards once again
gathered round

To tell about the places that each
had seen and found.

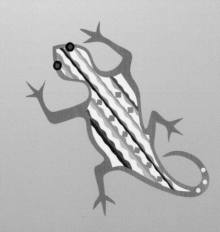

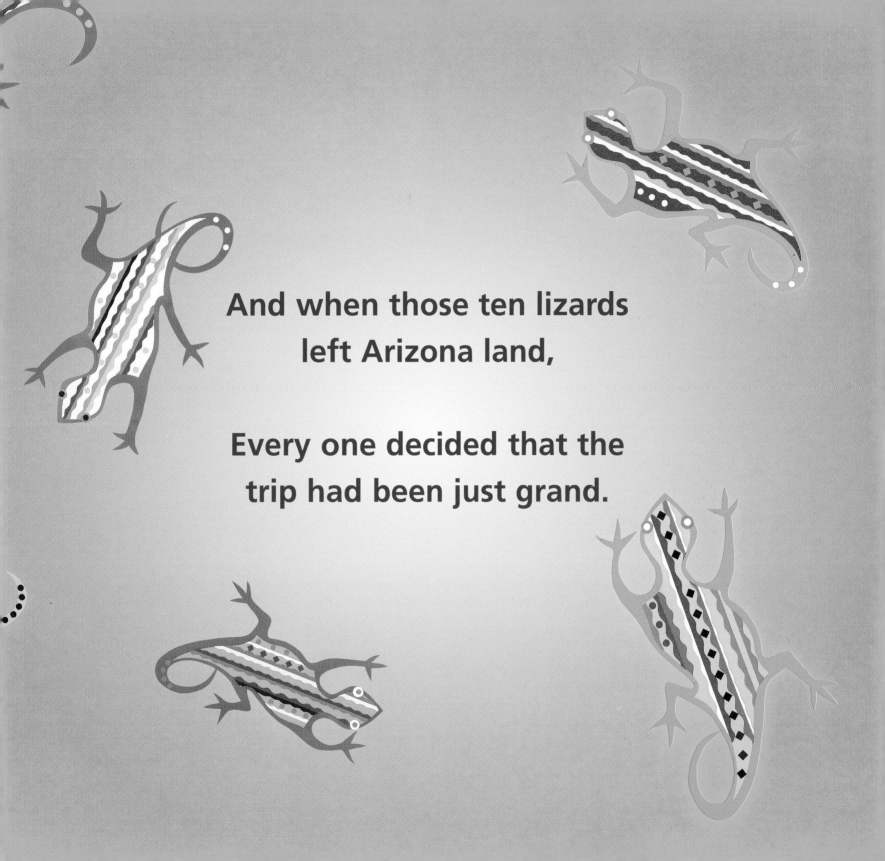

And when those ten lizards
left Arizona land,

Every one decided that the
trip had been just grand.

Resource Glossary for Parents and Teachers
of Each Arizona Treasure

(listed in the order mentioned in the story)

Copper Queen Mine—Copper has been one of Arizona's most important industries. From 1877 to 1975, this one mine produced more than 8 billion pounds of copper. Visitors can board an open train that has been converted to hold people instead of ore and ride 1800 feet into Copper Queen Mine for a tour that shows the way copper mining operated.

Sedona—An artistic community, Sedona is surrounded by beautiful red rock formations of cliffs and buttes. These red rocks stand out from the green trees and cactus, and photographers love to take pictures of the area. Many television shows and commercials have been filmed using Sedona's red rocks as a backdrop.

Snowbowl—Located in the San Francisco Peaks, seven miles north of Flagstaff, this resort offers wintertime sledding, cross country and downhill skiing. It has fifty-two runs/trails and five ski lifts. In the summer, visitors often take the one of the ski lifts for a Summer Scenic Skyride.

The Grand Canyon—The Grand Canyon is truly grand. Almost five million people a year come from throughout the world to visit the earth's greatest gorge. The Grand Canyon consists of more than a million acres of land. It is 277 miles long, 18 miles across at the widest spot, and more than one mile below the rim at the deepest spot. However, as large as the Grand Canyon is, it was not really known until 1869 when Major John Wesley Powell and his men traveled through it on small wooden boats.

Old Tucson—A re-creation of the Tucson of the 1880's with frontier buildings and wooden side-walks, Old Tucson has been the setting for 350 movies. Visitors can enjoy stunt shows, storytellers, and the singing and dancing at the saloon. Old Tucson also features a 128-year-old locomotive called the Reno.

Tombstone—Tombstone was made famous in many movies. Nicknamed "The Town too Tough to Die," it is known for the Boot Hill Graveyard, which holds the victims of the famous shootout at the OK Corral in 1881. People also visit The Birdcage Theater, where some of the bullets from sixteen gunfights still remain in the walls. Tombstone is also known for its rose tree, said to be the largest in the world.

Jerome—This old mining town was once called the "Wickedest in the West." A mining blast combined with shifting ground caused one whole block, including the town jail, to slide down a hill. When copper mining left the town, so did most of the people who lived there. Today, the population is only a small group of artists, but thousands of visitors now come to see one of the country's most popular ghost towns. The Jerome Inn, built in 1899, even calls one of its eight guest rooms "The Spooks, Ghosts, and Goblins."

London Bridge—London Bridge began to sink into the Thames, so the city of London sold it for 2.5 million dollars to the founder of Lake Havasu City, Robert P. Murdoch. He had the bridge dismantled, and the 10,276 granite blocks shipped from England. In Havasu, the bridge was put together piece by piece. It took three years and seven million dollars until completed in 1971. London Bridge now connects Lake Havasu City with an island in the lake and is a big tourist attraction.

Lake Powell—Though it is in the desert, this is the second largest man-made lake in the United States. It holds enough water to cover the whole state of Pennsylvania one foot deep. Five different rivers feed into Lake Powell, and it has 1960 miles of shoreline. Visitors enjoy swimming, water skiing, fishing, and boating, and especially living on a houseboat. The area is home to 170 species of birds and 800 different mammals.

Colossal Cave—Artifacts show that this cave was used about 1100 years ago by the Hohokam and later by the Apache. It is a maze that has never been completely explored. However, legends say that gold may be hidden within it. It is a dry cave and is one of the oldest established tourist attractions in Arizona. Some of the areas that visitors see have been named "The Crystal Forest," "The Living Room," and the "Kingdom of Elves." The temperature in the cave always remains around 70 degrees. The cave is located in Colossal Cave Mountain Park near Tucson.

Biosphere 2—Biosphere means sphere or ball of life. Biosphere 2 is 91 feet tall. The air and water are monitored every three minutes. When it began, eight people lived in the enclosed structure for two years. There are no plans for people to live there again, but visitors can tour Biosphere 2 with its distinct land types or biomes, including the largest human-made ocean. The purpose of Biosphere 2 is to provide scientists and students information about how to take better care of the earth.

Sabino Canyon—Located just northeast of Tucson, Sabino Canyon was first visited by hunters as long as twelve thousand years ago. Today, almost a million visitors a year enjoy the area's waterfalls and streams. Filled with saguaros and many other desert plants, the canyon is home to a lot of animal life. However, it's hard to see the animals because many blend into the landscape and they are much more active at night. No cars are allowed, but people may bike or hike or take the shuttle.

Petrified Forest National Park—This contains one of the largest and most colorful collections of petrified wood in the world. The 93,533 acres were a beautiful living rainforest 225 million years ago. Now the trees lie in flat sections of bright colored petrified wood. In the Rainbow Forest section, there is even an old sixteenth century Indian hut made of petrified wood.

Kartchner Caverns State Park—Discovered in 1974, this is one of the few live caves in the world. Water still percolates from the surface, growing calcite formations. One soda straw stalactite is 21 feet long and still growing. Human visitors can tour the cave. However, one room is closed during the time thousands of bats visit.

Phoenix Zoo—Covering 125 acres, this zoo is home to more than 1300 animals. There are four main trails to follow through the zoo: Africa with baboons, rhinos, and lions; Arizona with coyotes, gila monsters, and rattlesnakes; Discovery where children can interact with domestic animals, and Tropics where visitors can explore the Forest of Uco.

Heard Museum—Located in Phoenix, The Heard has ten exhibit galleries of Native American art and culture. In addition to many adult visitors, 25,000 school children visit this museum each year. One additional feature is a working artist's studio which encourages interaction between visitors and Native American artists.

Arizona Science Center—A five-story IMAX theater here can make viewers feel as if they are in the movie they are watching. Arizona Science Center also has a planetarium with interactive armrests that give visitors a chance to feel a part of the night skies. However, the main attraction of this Phoenix museum is the 300 hands-on exhibits in five themed areas.

Walnut Canyon—The Sinagua Indian tribe lived here over 900 years ago. People can still climb down in the canyon to see more than twenty-five of the Sinagua's cliff homes. These ancient homes provided both heat and safety. Their southeast exposure provided solar heating, and the cliff location made it very difficult for any outsider to attack. Located near Flagstaff, the canyon mixes different lifezones. Visitors see desert cacti growing next to mountain firs.

Phoenix—The capital of Arizona is one of the seven largest cities in the United States and is located in the north-central part of the state. The climate is warm and sunny, averaging 300 days of sunshine each year and only seven inches of rain. The city of Phoenix is built on the site of the Hohokam ancient ruins and is named after the legend of the Phoenix bird. This fantastic bird was supposed to have lived for 500 years and at the end of its life, burned itself in a fire. From the ashes, a new Phoenix bird arose.

Lake Powell

Grand Canyon

Petrified Forest
National Park

Walnut Canyon

Snow Bowl Ski Resort

London Bridge

Jerome

Sedona

Arizona Science
Center

Heard Museum

Phoenix Zoo

Sabino Canyon

Biosphere 2

Old Tucson

Colossal Cave

Tombstone

Kartchner Caverns

Copper
Queen
Mine

An award-winning author, TERRI FIELDS has lived in Arizona for over thirty years and loves sharing all the great aspects of the state with newcomers.

She has written sixteen books and has been able to visit with students throughout the United States about her work as an author. She has even been invited to Japan and Morocco and personally presented her books to students in those countries as well.

In addition to writing, Terri is also an educator who has been named Arizona Teacher of the Year and U S WEST Outstanding Arizona Teacher, and has been selected as one of the teachers on the All-USA Teacher Team of the nation's top educators.

TONY MARINELLA is a freelance photographer living in Flagstaff, Arizona with his wife Amy and son Thomas. He is widely published in national newspapers, magazines, calendars, postcards, and books.

Tony's passion for photography began at the age of fourteen when a family friend gave him his first camera. He began his professional carrier in 1992 after completing a degree in photography at Northern Arizona University.

Tony's images cover a wide variety of subjects including the southwest landscape, nature and action sports. This is Tony's first children's book, dedicated to his son Thomas, who is featured on the last page of the book.

The lizards, created from cut paper, were designed by GERARD TSONAKWA, a Native American artist and author who resides in Tucson, Arizona.